Looking Beyond The Sky

By SALLY BETTERS

Illustrated by LINDA LLOYD

To children young and old who ponder the beauty of creation and wonder what lies beyond the sky.

— Sally Betters

May the words and illustrations of this book reach those little ones whom God loves and keeps watch over.

— Linda Lloyd

Book Design and Production by Lynn Caprarelli
ISBN: 9798588654241

SPECIAL THANKS

I want to extend a wholehearted thank you to the following committed family and friends. My heart is full with your generous gestures of kindness, skills, and talents. Your prayers, donations and words of encouragement are a valuable part of this book.

Richard Betters, Edmund N. Sanchez, Arcy Torres, Arcy Piña,
Dr. Edward Piña, Willa Gardea, Mary Jane López, Steve López,
Linda Lloyd, Lynn Caprarelli, Kathy Johnson, Nanette O'Neal,
Traci Harris, Carole Boersma, Jeanette Edwards, Julie Ann Cooper,
Roberta Bryer-King, Renee Vidor, Peggy Hinman, Donna Cowan,
Anita M. McLaurin, Michael and Kristine Freedman, Pat Weaver,
Dan Broyles, Linda and James Mendel, and Kathy Cox

Have you ever sat looking up at the big, beautiful, blue, sky,

and wondered if God lives way up high?

Do your eyes sparkle with joy at the sun—winged birds,

who gracefully glide without any words?

Have you ever tasted raindrops on the tip of your tongue,

or held snow in your hands, making them numb?

Does your heart
dance when you hear the
waves of the ocean,

crashing loudly with
spectacular motion?

Can you hear the rustling sounds of a powerful breeze, dancing through the trees and twirling the leaves?

Do you ever marvel at the colors of a warm, sherbet, sunset, watching the sun disappear like a picture you will never forget?

Sometimes the days are not fun and free.

Our feelings are mixed up like a twisted, tangled tree.

What do you do when
your heart is sad?

Do you push it aside and
get really mad?

Is there a person you trust
to talk with and share?

Do they listen?
Do they seem to care?

Your feelings are important, so please share your heart; this helps when you're lonely to give a new start.

When someone
has hurt you and you
don't know what to do;
it's important to tell
someone who will help
and protect you.

You are not alone in this uncomfortable place.

There are people who care and will give you some grace.

Soon you'll feel better and enjoy the wonder all around you today.

You don't want to miss the golden moments that can drift away.

So keep looking up,
and give God thanks
for each new day.
There are many good
things coming your way.

ABOUT THE AUTHOR

Sally Betters is a published author of the award-nominated nonfiction book, *From Crisis to Compassion. Looking Beyond the Sky*, is her debut as a children's author. Her passion to serve others with her skills, time, and talents show through in her writing, speaking and life coaching. She lives in a quaint mountain community with the love of her life: her husband, Richard. Sally is a proud mother of two amazing sons, and a grandmother of five kind, loving, and intelligent granddaughters. You can contact Sally through her website at www.sallybetters.com.

Made in the USA
Las Vegas, NV
28 January 2021